DATE DUE

AUG 2 2 1995		
FEB 0 7 1996		

Prelude

One fine winter day, a happy-go-lucky young man named Jack was strolling down the road, feeling a little hungry. Suddenly, he was surprised to meet an old man he had never seen before. In one hand the man held a long staff; in the other were 2 large golden seeds. "I am a wizard," the old man said, "and I have something for you...."

ANNO'S MAGIC SEEDS

written and illustrated by
MITSUMASA ANNO

Philomel Books

New York

The wizard handed Jack the 2 golden seeds. "These are magic,"
he said. "Bake 1 seed in the oven until it is red and then eat it.
You will not be hungry again for a whole year. Bury the other seed
in the ground now and care for it well. I promise you it will grow
and give you 2 more magic seeds in the fall."
Jack did exactly what the wizard
told him to do.

The next spring, 1 tiny sprout came up.
It grew and grew into a sturdy plant.

In the summer, 2 beautiful flowers bloomed on the plant.
A little later, 2 fruits appeared where the flowers had been.

And in the fall, the 2 marvelous fruits produced 2 seeds,
just like those the wizard had given him.

In the winter, Jack baked 1 seed to eat,
and buried the other in the ground.

The next spring came. Just as before,
1 tiny plant grew from the seed Jack had buried.

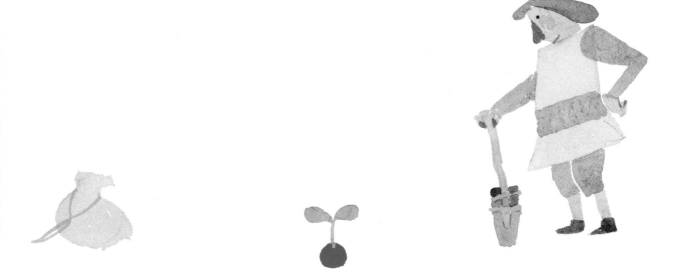

Summer came. 2 beautiful flowers bloomed on the
plant, followed by 2 marvelous fruits.

Fall came. And again,
the marvelous fruits produced 2 seeds.

In the winter, Jack ate 1 baked seed
and buried the other seed in the ground.

Once again, in the year after this, 1 plant came up and 2 flowers bloomed and 2 marvelous fruits grew and 2 seeds were made. And again, Jack ate 1 seed and buried the other.

The next year, the flowers bloomed again and the marvelous fruits grew and 2 seeds were made, just as before. Again, Jack baked 1 seed and ate it and buried the other seed in the ground.

The next year, while Jack rested and watched, a plant came up, flowers bloomed on it, then 2 fruits appeared and 2 seeds were made. And as before, Jack ate 1 seed and buried the other in the ground.

And in the next year after that, the flowers bloomed and the marvelous fruits grew and the 2 seeds were produced as well. Again, Jack ate 1 seed and buried the other.

But finally, Jack began to think about it. "This can just go on and on in the same way forever," he said to himself, "if I just go on doing the same thing every year. Well, this year I will bury *both* seeds in the ground.

"I will get through the winter somehow, by eating something different."
So, that winter, he buried 2 seeds in the ground. He tended them very carefully.

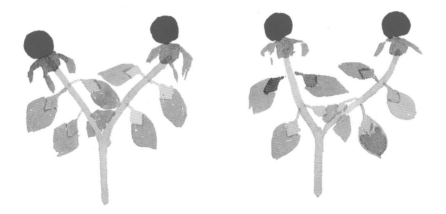

The next year—that is, the *first* year after he planted both seeds—what do you think happened? In the spring, 2 sprouts came up, and in the fall, 4 seeds were produced. In the winter, Jack baked and ate 1 seed and buried the other 3 seeds in the ground.

← *noisemaker*

Then, in the spring of the *second* year after his discovery, 3 sprouts came up. And in the fall, 6 seeds were made. That winter, Jack ate 1 seed and buried the other 5. He made a noisemaker to scare away crows and sparrows, so they wouldn't come and eat the seeds. When the wind blew on it, the noise it made startled the birds.

How many fruits will grow in Jack's garden next fall?

Well, the next year—that is, the *third* year
after he got the idea—all the sprouts came up
in the spring. And in the fall, 10 seeds were
made from the 10 marvelous fruits.

In the winter, Jack buried 9 seeds in
the ground. He baked 1 seed and ate it.

The next year, the *fourth* year, in the spring there came
the sprouts, and in the fall there were 18 seeds. That
winter, Jack buried 17 seeds in the ground.

The next year—that is, the *fifth* year—in the spring all the sprouts came up, and in the fall the new seeds were made. That winter, Jack ate 1 seed and he buried the rest of them in the ground.

How many seeds did he bury?

The next year, the *sixth*,
all the sprouts came up, just as before.
And that fall many seeds grew, so many that
Jack didn't bother to count them anymore.
While he was busy gathering in his harvest of seeds,
a nice young woman came along. Her name was Alice.
Alice stopped to help him.

How many seeds grew that year?

Jack ate 1 baked seed and so did Alice.
And that winter, they buried the rest
of the seeds in the ground.

How many seeds did they bury?

In the spring of the next year, the *seventh* year, all the sprouts came up, and in the fall there were many seeds from all the fruits. That winter, Jack and Alice got married and held a wedding party. They gave 2 delicious magic seeds to each of their 5 guests. Each guest saved 1 seed for a souvenir of this happy day. Jack and Alice ate 1 seed each.

That year they also built a little storehouse and put 16 seeds in it to keep for a while. The rest of the seeds they buried in the ground.

How many seeds did they bury?

The next spring, the *eighth*,
a lot of sprouts came up, and
in the fall many seeds appeared.
And then, because they had quite
enough seeds, they decided to
sell some at the town market.

They took 60 seeds to sell, including all those that they had put in the storehouse
the year before. Then they put 34 new seeds in the storehouse, set aside 1 seed each
to eat and buried all the rest of the seeds in the ground.

*How many seeds
did they bury in the ground?*

The next year was the *ninth* since Jack had had his good idea.

In the spring a lot of sprouts came up, and in the fall a lot of seeds were made. That year their baby was born. So in the winter 3 seeds were eaten, since each of them ate 1 seed. Now, because they had so many seeds, they went to the market to sell 100 of them, including all those they had been keeping in their storehouse. They put 51 of the new crop of seeds into the storehouse and buried all the rest of the seeds in their field.

How many?

The next year was the *tenth*. The baby was growing, so Jack and Alice built a new, bigger house. In the fall, their field was filled with plants bearing the magic seeds. Soon it would be time for gathering in their harvest.

But suddenly: "Oh!" said Jack. "The wind is blowing awfully hard!"

It was a hurricane!
They had never expected such a terrible storm.
The river overran its banks and soon there was a flood.

Jack tied the house firmly to a tree, so it would not be carried away.
Then he pulled the cow up onto their cart, which was now floating like a ship.
Alice, holding their little boy in her arms, ran up to the attic of the house.
Jack managed to scoop up a small bag of seeds. He tied the bag to the tree.

What a dreadful storm it was!
The wind shook the trees and blew the rain against them.
Soon the field looked just like a wild sea.
The wind roared and the dark, muddy water rumbled and rolled over the plants.
The crops and the storehouse were completely washed away.

Finally, the storm was over. The sky cleared and the sun came out. But the fields were empty and bare.

"Still, our baby is safe. I am glad for that," said Alice.
"So am I, very glad indeed," said Jack. "And our cow has survived and I was able to save 10 seeds. So cheer up, dear wife. We will start all over and make a new life together."

Jack baked 3 seeds. He gave 1 seed to Alice and 1 to their child and he ate 1 seed himself. He buried the rest of the seeds in the ground.

Jack and his wife then bowed their heads
and prayed together for a good crop.

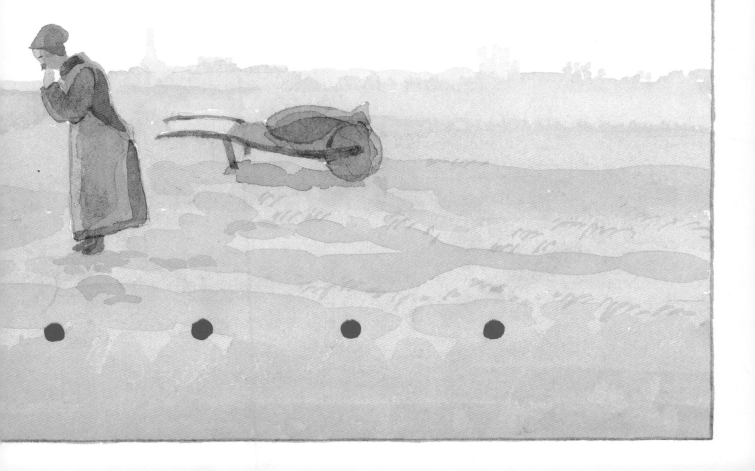

A Note From Mitsumasa Anno

I called this book *The Magic Seeds* because, in fact, there is a mysterious power in even one tiny seed that seems quite beyond our understanding. Of course, we could not live for a year on one grain of rice or cereal, as Jack did. But if we should bury one seed in the ground and take care of the plant that grows from it, it would not be long before we had a crop of hundreds of thousands of grains. In our real world of nature there are many such magical events—more than are contained in all the most fantastic picture books.

A long, long time ago, human beings learned to grow plants for their food and other needs. They sowed seeds in the ground and fertilized them; they protected their growing plants from harmful birds and insects. They prayed to God for rain. And when their harvest produced more food than they needed, commerce and trade began, and calculating and bargaining and other things we may think of as typical of civilization. And then, unfortunately, some people began to quarrel and fight with each other.

I don't mean to refer in this book to all of these difficult matters. Yet I think you will find that many events in our real world are quite a lot like things that happen in this story. I hope you will find this interesting.

English language translation copyright © 1995 by Philomel Books. Original edition copyright © 1992 by Kūsō Kōbō.
All rights reserved. This book, or parts thereof, may not be reproduced in any form without permission in writing from the publisher.
First American edition published in 1995 by Philomel Books, a division of The Putnam & Grosset Group,
200 Madison Avenue, New York, NY 10016.
Philomel Books, Reg. U.S. Pat. & Tm. Off. Originally published in Japanese in 1992 by Dowaya Publishing Co.,
Tokyo, under the title *Fushigina Tane*. English translation rights arranged with Dowaya, through Japan Foreign-Rights Center.
Published simultaneously in Canada. Printed in Singapore.
Type design by Songhee Kim. Text set in Goudy Old Style.
Library of Congress Cataloging-in-Publication Data
Anno, Mitsumasa, 1926-   Anno's magic seeds / by Mitsumasa Anno.   p.   cm.
Summary: The reader is asked to perform a series of mathematical operations integrated into the story of a man
who plants magic seeds and reaps an increasingly abundant harvest.
1. Arithmetic series—Juvenile literature. 2. Mathematical recreations—Juvenile literature. [1. Arithmetic. 2. Mathematical
recreations.] I. Title.   QA295.A66 1995   92-39309   CIP   AC   513'.4—dc20
ISBN 0-399-22538-2

10 9 8 7 6 5 4 3 2 1

First Philomel edition